The Femininity Factor

Thomika Bridwell

Dedication

All Great Truths Begin as Blasphemies- George Bernard Shaw

My Darling daughter, may you live your truth so unapologetically that you have the distinct honor of being called blasphemous.

Table of Contents

Allow Me to Reintroduce Myself

Dear One,

How have you been? I've tried reaching you several time and so far, my efforts have been unsuccessful. I'm not telling you this because I'm thinking of giving up on you; on us. I'm really just writing because I wanted you to know that I miss you....

I actually thought that I saw you out the other day. In fact, I'm certain that it was you. I watched in the distance but you looked so busy; so, involved in what you were doing that I didn't want to interrupt your flow. I stood there and just watched for a moment (I didn't want to be a complete creep) and admittedly, was filled with so many questions.

It's so weird, there was a time when we were so close. Inseparable. I could say without a doubt that I knew everything there was to know about you. But as I watched in the distance, I realized how much of your life has become a mystery to me.... But there you were. with your children and definitely preoccupied, so I didn't think it was a good time to engage you. My solution, this letter.... That way you could just read when you had a moment to yourself (I Know how you hate to bombarded out of the blue) ... And I thought it would also give us a chance to have a long overdue conversation. One that we could open up the lines of communication and speak to each other beyond the niceties. But, a real conversation. A conversation based in truth. A conversation where I could ask you the hard questions without the awkwardness and distance that time, life, and people has forged in our union....

But, Like I said in the beginning. I'll never give up on us. And our journey together is not a sprint. It is indeed, a marathon. I just wanted to take the first step and let you know that I'm still here. No matter how much time passes, I'm here.... Ours is a destiny written in the stars. And even when it seems we are too far gone, that could not be further from the truth.

 I completely understand that your life has taken many turns. I actually look forward to hearing about all of your varied experiences. I could tell as I watched you skillfully multi task, that you have many things that you are involved in. Things that pull your energy in many different directions. Things that fill your time, and parts of your life. But, maybe are taking up more time than you intended. And have left little room for you.... This is not in any way a judgement on that. Nor is it an attempt to pull you away from your other obligations. Your other relationships. I just wanted to remind you of our relationship and that I need you too.... I will be bold enough to say that we need each other. And if we look at the state of the world, I'd be remised if I didn't say that the world has need of what's inside of you.

You know that I don't believe in coincidence and I know that seeing you after all these years wasn't just an isolated incident. I knew it would happen when it was time. Time for you to remember. Time for us to realign.... Now is the time! Did you miss me?

Love,

Purpose

The American Dream

Two weeks Jacobo thought as he laid face up to the ceiling. Jacobo was in shock. He really didn't think this day would come. Ever since their parents had left to the states, all they talked about was the day they leave— but together.

"Eyyy, you up?" Juan Pablo whispered over to Jacobo. He didn't want to wake up Altagracia and Nina.

After a long pause, Jacobo replies "yea, what's up?"

"I can't sleep. I'm too excited, my heart just keeps racing faster and faster".

"You still have two weeks to go loco. Can't drop dead before then".

"You're stupid" Juan Pablo laughed.

"Shhh!" Altagracia hushed them from the living room.

"Sorry mama" Juan Pablo replied.

"I just have so much to do still, you know?" Juan Pablo continued despite his grandmothers warning.

"Like what?" Jacobo replied perplexed.

What could he possibly need to do? It's not like he can take much on this damn trip. Jacobo thought to himself.

"Well for starters I haven't even told Minerva I'm leaving".

"What?!" Jacobo bolted.

"Cono!" Altagracia yelled from the living room. "If y'all make me get up from this bed I'll whip you both. It's two in the morning! Y'all think I still won't hit y'all cuz y'all grown?"

Jacobo and Juan Pablo widened their eyes as they sank in bed. Neither one replied. They knew these were all rhetorical questions. That if they did answer, they'd get whooped for being disrespectful.

"We'll finish this tomorrow bro, goodnight". Juan Pablo whispered turning away from Jacobo".

"Nite".

"Platano, Maduro, Aguacate!, Platano, Maduro, Aguacate!".

"These damn people never let us sleep" Jacobo said after being woken up by the street vendor.

He gets up from his bed and makes his way to the outhouse. With a blue gallon cup in half in one hand and his toothbrush and paste in another. Out back he reached into one of the 3 water containers to fill the gallon in hand. Squatting down he takes a gulp of water and begins swishing it around his mouth. Spits it out and begins to brush his teeth. From the corner of his eye he sees his grandmother approaching him.

"Sorry we kept you up mama" Jacobo mumbled with his toothbrush still in his mouth.

4

"Ayy please. That's nothing, try going through this with all of you for over 40 years!"

Juan Pablo laughed and rinsed his mouth. "Mijo, we have no aguacate. Go catch that vendor and bring me back three GOOD aguacates. Que esten Maduros"

"Mama, he been left".

"Better get to it then" Altagracia replied with her infamous smirk.

Jacobo goes back into the room, but Juan Pablo has already left. *Where'd he go.*

"Saludos Vecina" Jacobo greeted his neighbor on his way out. Vere was always sitting outside. She's older and has trouble getting around on her own, so she just waits around for her daughter who cares for her.

Jacobo stands in the middle of the street to try to catch a glimpse of the vendor, but can't find him.

Shit, I'm gonna have to walk all the way down to the market. But then he sees Juan Pablo holding up four aguacates.

"Of course" Jacobo replied laughing back at his brother. "You are truly something else man".

"You know I always got you" Juan Pablo reassured.

"I know, I'm gonna miss you man"

Juan Pablo wrapped his arm around his brother and kissed his forehead.

"Ok get the fuck out of here with all that" Jacobo said pushing his brother off. "You and your funky ass. You didn't even brush your teeth".

"Ok, relax, I was looking out for you bro".

"I know" Jacobo replied mournfully.

"Here we go, don't start Jaco, lets go see what mama made for breakfast".

"Right because the bread and butter varies" Jacobo said sarcastically.

"There he is! That's more like you".

La Novia

To Jacobo's surprise, mama had pastelitos for breakfast, not just bread this morning.

"Wepa! What are we celebrating?" Jacobo joked.

"Hey don't be silly. We have to be grateful" Altagracia replied as she lay their plates out on the table.

"So, about last night. What is all this you still have to do before you leave?" Jacobo asked Juan Pablo.

"Leave? Leave where? Where you going?" Altagracia questioned.

Juan Pablo grinned at his brother. He was mad, but at the same time felt relieved. *One less person to go* he thought.

"My bad bro" Jacobo added,

"It's all good, don't even sweat it".

"Mama, I'm leaving to the states, I was waiting until everything was finalized to tell you".

"Finalized? This all sounds finalized to me. Do your parents know?" Altagracia asked.

"Well that's what Jaco is asking. I still have a some things to take care of, I still have to tell a couple of people. Everything just happened so fast mama. The cayote called last week and said someone from this month's trip had backed out. They had one more spot open. I jumped at the opportunity".

"It's ok mijo. This is what you've been working so hard for. If this opportunity came without you seeking it, know that God is with you".

"Thanks mama. He is, but please don't mention any of this to Carla when she comes by later. I've planned a nice dinner for us. I don't just want to drop the news on her like this".

"What fancy dinner can you afford? You better save every peso!"

Juan Pablo almost spit out his coffee laughing. I'm gonna miss your sarcasm. Getting up from his chair he leaned over her full set of gray and kissed the crown of her head.

"I'm taking her to Dona Olivia's house. You know she has that nice galleria. She agreed to host us when I told her I was leaving".

"Don't you have any shame, how dare you ask to use someone elses home?"

"Mama you know it's not like that. I've been working for Dona Olivia for over 10 years. To her like the son she never had and to your point I did offer to pay her, but she laughed in my face. Won't even let me buy the ingredients for the meal".

Altagracia stared at him shacking her head. *This little boy is always plotting. He's always been able to charm his way around with that big smile of his.* Although she felt a gapping hole in the pit of her stomach, this mere thought brought her peace. She knew in heart that if anyone would make it in New York it'll be Juan Pablo.

Ever since he was six, he went knocking on neighbors' doors asking what they needed help with. He started off just running *colmado* errands, grabbing a pound of flour or cheese for Dona Olivia here and there, buying cigarettes for the neighborhood drunks who were too lazy or intoxicated to walk down the street by themselves. He would only get a couple of cents per run, but that didn't stop him. Juan Pablo knew that if he'd continue, soon these pennies would add up.

When people tried to pay clothes or other knick-knacks, he'd kindly decline. Growing up in this poverty-stricken neighborhood had taught Juan Pablo early on that money solves problems, not fancy clothes. It's the reason both of his parents worked so hard.

"I don't know why you're so money hungry son" his father would say every time he saw his son running around frantically. "If you keep going at this rate, you'll have no energy to work once you get to be my age. So just take it easy my boy". But there wasn't a soul on Earth that could tame Juan Pablo's ambition.

Everyone knew who Juan Pablo was, or *el hijo de Vicente* as he was most commonly referred to. By the age of ten Juan Pablo was patching up holes, painting, replacing broken window shutters. All of the neighbors were impressed with how diligent this little boy was. There was never a job he said no to and if he didn't know how to fix something, he'd figure it out.

"Don't be like that, you know I'm doing all of this for you mama. You deserve better than this tiny one bedroom. Look at how cramped we are. You think I like seeing you share a bed with _____? You've worked too hard raising us for us not to work harder for you now".

"Ehh, you know I don't need much". Altagracia dismissed him. She felt grievance in her heart but would never show it. Her little firecracker would soon be gone, and she couldn't stomach the thought.

"You ok mama?" Jacobo asked sensing her diminishing spirits.

"Claro, you want more café?" she asked.

"No thanks".

Adios

"When's this fancy dinner (look up famous actor at the time)?"

"Tonight. I'm actually nervous believe it or not".

"Ohh I belivve you brother. You think I haven't seen Carla in action? That's why I was so surprised you haven't told her".

"I know. But you know how possessive she is. Just thinking about telling her makes my stomach turn. She's never been ok with us leaving, even planning to leave. So imagine. She keeps thinks we'll get hurt like mami did that time they robbed the store. She doesn't understand how I need to be there to protect them both. If I was at the store that night mami wouldn't of gotten assaulted".

"Damn bro, sounds like you

]

Cayote

Vicente and Altagracia were in their late 30's when they first set foot in New York. Young immigrants eager to get started on their new business venture. Ready to put their life's savings to work. Desperate to help their family back home in Bani. They had no idea how quickly New York would suck out that dream and twist it into a nightmare.

America

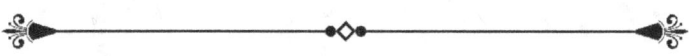

Nueva Yol

Radame

Restaurant Alta Mar

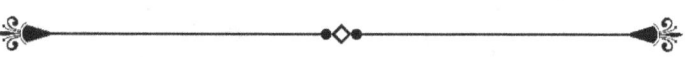

La Pinta

Family Bonds

Cooking Rocks

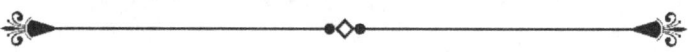

Just Say No

Another Day in the Hood

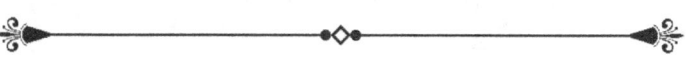

Corrupt Cops

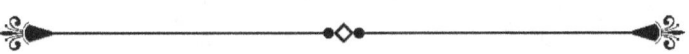

Break Down

Lock Up

First Visit

Last Letter

Deportation

Las Americas